The Laughing Rive

a folktale for peace

Elizabeth Haze Vega

Rayve Productions Inc.
Windsor CA

To:
dam + Kevin
May you both
enjoy the story
+ the musical
C.D.

Love,
Auntie Eleanor
& Uncle Joe

Rayve Productions Inc.
Box 726   Windsor CA 95492 USA

Print production coordinator: Kim McDonell
Printed in Korea through Pan Pacific Graphics, San Ramon

Publisher's Cataloging in Publication
  Vega, Elizabeth Haze.
  The laughing river: a folktale for peace
  by Elizabeth Haze Vega; illustrated by Ashley Smith
  p. cm. -- (Folktales for peace; v. 1)
  ISBN 1-877810-35-5 (book)
  ISBN 1-877810-36-3 (audio music tape)
  ISBN 1-877810-37-1 (kit)

  SUMMARY: Lyrical folktale concerning two African tribes in conflict
who are brought together by a melodious, laughing river. Incorporates
accurate musical notes which create a song by story's end into the
illustrations and text.

  1. Rivers--Juvenile fiction. 2. Peace--Juvenile fiction. 3. Music--Juvenile fiction.
4. Dancing--Juvenile fiction. 5. Drum--Juvenile fiction. I. Smith, Ashley, ill. II. Title. III. Series.

PZ7.V443Laug 1995   [E]

Library of Congress Catalog Card Number 94-69051

Contents

This book is dedicated

with love

to

my parents,

Bill and Betty Hayes

my husband,

Bobby Vega

and

The children of the 21st century

The Birth of a Folktale

With gratitude to all who contributed

The story you are about to hear, see, read and play is a modern folktale with origins born in African history. A mesmerizing African folksong is the seed from which the story grew.

The Laughing River was inspired by, and evolved from, many sources, each of which I greatly appreciate. Janet Greene, an Orff music instructor from California, developed the concept of conflict between two fictitious tribes, the Funga and the Alafia, from a West African Yoruba greeting song, **Funga Alafia.** Adding words of peace taught by Professor Jos Wuytack, a Belgian Orff instructor, the story grew. Orff students dramatized and expounded upon the story line.

I nurtured these ingredients, mixed them around, added other songs, rearranged the music and story line, and adapted them to accommodate the instruments and voices of my students at Wee Rock School of Music. My "youngest critics" at Wee Rock School and elsewhere played a vital role during the developmental phase of the **Laughing River** project; their enthusiasm, responses, and suggestions served as practical guides for my work in progress.

When the written story was complete, New Zealand artist Ashley Smith set to work, and through his vibrant, fun-filled illustrations, the exotic and colorful world of the Funga and Alafia tribes took shape.

Meanwhile, in the studios of Free Mountain Music in Novato, California, under the technical guidance of David Freiberg and the production assistance of Bobby Vega, the story was given the breath of life, captured in time and space, and recorded for children of all ages.

One more dimension materialized with the **Laughing River** drum-building project — a frame drum inspired by a traditional African instrument. I, along with other Orff students, was introduced to a variation of the African drum by Orff instructor, Craig Woodson. Over a number of years, I further modified the drum for today's children, who I hope will build and play this instrument, adding the heartbeat to our living, growing folktale.

The labor of love which brought all of these elements together could not have been accomplished without the vision, encouragement and guidance of Rayve Productions. Norm and Barbara Ray nurtured and supported the author and the work and played a major role in the birth of this folktale — **The Laughing River.**

—Elizabeth Haze Vega

The Laughing River —
African Threads Past and Present

Tribal Representation: The Laughing River is a blend of several fascinating African elements. It was inspired by an African greeting song in the Yoruba language, which is spoken in Yorubaland, a West African area within Nigeria that is inhabited by a number of different tribes. The fictitious tribes, the "Alafia" and the "Funga," are modeled after the Yoruba people, particularly the Oyo. Inspiration was also drawn from the religious beliefs of the Bunu tribe, who occupy a region in Northern Nigeria. The song, **Che Che Koolay**, (page 20) originated in Ghana.

Weaving, A Gift of the Spirit World: In Yoruban culture, the art of weaving is considered a gift from the spirit world. Before Chrisitanity was introduced into West Africa, great value — social, economic and spiritual — was placed on the production of handwoven and handspun cloth. In **The Laughing River**, Funga and Alafia people wear brightly patterned garments; these colors and patterns hold significant meaning for the Yoruba. Historically, the Yoruba have created intricately designed, richly colored, woven fabric, and they continue this traditional practice today. However, in keeping with the 1990s, the Yoruba now incorporate modern symbols into their weaving. On page 9, Funga women wear clothing featuring patterns of "modern tradition" — **gento**, a roguish university student; **groto**, a sugar daddy; and **yamoussoukro**, a paved road or highway.

On page 11, an Alafia woman weaves a pattern called **Dallas**, whose roots are deep in the heart of Texas . . . and American television. All these patterns connect with the present while paying homage to the traditions and values of the past.

Water and Womanhood: To the Yoruba, water and the spirit world are closely associated, a feature that is significant in **The Laughing River**. Although the correlation is not directly drawn within the context of the story, it is implied that the power to overcome anger and aggression lies within the river.

The Bunu also view the spirit world as the source of women's fertility. A direct translation of the word áshe, (Funga Alafia Song, page 22) is a spiritual command, calling upon the power to create, or make things happen. The river is a symbolic representation of the power of áshe. Bunu villagers associate the underwater spirit world with a religious group known as **Ejinuwon**. **Eji** means child, and **nuwon** means water; literally, "children of the water." In **The Laughing River**, the Alafia people laugh, sing and swim in the river, drenching themselves in the power of **áshe**, through which they are given the power to create a new relationship with their aggressive neighbors.

Power for Peace: The Laughing River is a story of conflict between peoples — a scenario all too common in our world. It is also a story of conflict resolution and peace. I hope that this story will inspire all who read or hear it, fill them with a desire for peace, and empower them with áshe, the strength to create peace in our world.

♡ ♡ ♡

A Note About Orff Music

The instruments you hear on **The Laughing River** audiocassette are Orff instruments. Carl Orff (1895—1982) was an Austrian composer who developed a holistic approach to teaching music which uses these pitched percussion instruments. These xylophones, metallophones and glockenspiels are adaptations of African marimba/xylophones and the Balinese gamelan.

With the capacity to remove notes, these instruments are often tuned to pentatonic scales. By removing the dissonant intervals, children are given the freedom to experiment and improvise while creating pleasing harmonic sounds.

The Orff approach addresses different learning styles by allowing students to experience music on many different levels. The rhythm of the spoken word is often a starting point for teaching children a musical concept. Integrating movements, speech, songs, games, instruments, dramatics and more, the Orff approach is a delightful way to experience the Magic of Music!

— Elizabeth Haze Vega

Orff Instruments

BB:	Bass Bars
BX:	Bass Xylophone
AX:	Alto Xylophone
AM:	Alto Metallophone
AG:	Alto Glockenspiel
SG:	Soprano Glockenspiel

Once upon a time not so very long ago, on a far away continent, there was a beautiful country. And in the middle of this country was the most magnificent mountain you have ever seen.

Now in the forest beneath the mountain there lived a very proud and beautiful tribe of people. They were called the Funga people. 𝄢 Well, the Funga people were very strong and brave. They had much to be proud of. They carved beautiful drums from the trees which grew in their forest. All the people played the drums and they would compete to see who was the best among them.

They were also strong and tall and could run very fast; and they would hold competitions to see who could throw the farthest, or run the fastest, or jump the highest. But they were always arguing and bickering with one another about this thing or that. ♪ All day long their angry voices would echo off of the mountain.

Now
in this very same land
there ran a long and lazy river. ♪1
All day long the water bubbled and laughed
as it made its way through the valley and the forests. ♪2
On the banks of this river there lived another tribe of people and they
were called the Alafia people. ♪3 The Alafia were a happy tribe. All day long they
sang and laughed as they wove their fishing nets and painted their beautiful fishing canoes.
The Alafia children played in the sun and swam in the laughing river. At night they would gather together
to dance and sing.

#1
AM

"La, la, la, Alafia, hey, hey, hey, la.

La, la, la, Alafia, hey, hey, hey, hey, la."

The sound of their music and their happy voices floated
over the river and echoed off of the great mountain,
right into the village of the Funga people.

#2
AX

Now this made the Funga tribe very angry.

"How can we sleep?"
"We need our rest so that we can hunt in the early morning."

They argued and argued about what to do.

Finally, the chief told his best drummers
to call all the people together;
and the drums echoed
from the mountain.

Soon,
all of the Funga people
were gathered together around the fire.

"Tonight," said the chief, "we will put an end
to all this racket. This very night we will
raid their village and teach the Alafia people a lesson.

Prepare yourselves!"

And so, when the moon rose high over the mountain,
and the happy voices of the Alafia people were heard floating
over the laughing waters, the Funga tribe
set out from their village
and crept to the
river's edge.

Slowly they began to make their way across the river.
But as each person stepped into the water,
the happy river rushed between their toes
and began to tickle their feet.
Soon the whole tribe was
laughing and falling
into the water.

When the Alafia people heard all the commotion,
they ran quickly to the banks of the river.

"Ah, you have come to join our party," they called;
and they sang out their welcome song.

" I greet you with my mind,
I greet you with my lips,
I greet you with my heart,
and I have no weapons.

I greet you with my mind,
I greet you with my lips,
I greet you with my heart,
and I have no weapons."

"Che, che, koolay.

    (echo) Che, che, koolay.

Che, che, ko, fe, sa.

    (echo) Che, che, ko, fe, sa.

Ko fe salanga.

    (echo) Ko fe salanga.

Ga ga [or la ga] shelanga.

    (echo) Ga ga shelanga.

Kum, eh, deh, deh.

    (echo) Kum, eh, deh, deh.

Kum, eh, deh, deh.

    (echo) Kum, eh, deh, deh.

Kum, eh, deh, deh.

    (echo) Kum, eh, deh, deh.

Kum, kum, kum."

Now when the Funga people heard the welcome song, they were no longer afraid
or angry at the Alafia tribe; in fact, they liked them very much,
and they began to play their drums and sing together.

"Funga [or 'funwa'] Alafia, áshe, áshe.
Funga Alafia, áshe, áshe.

Funga Alafia, áshe, áshe.
Funga Alafia, áshe, áshe."

Translation

"Let there be peace, so be it (amen), so be it (amen).
Let there be peace, so be it (amen), so be it (amen).

Let there be peace, so be it (amen), so be it (amen).
Let there be peace, so be it (amen), so be it (amen).

And this is how the Funga people and the Alafia people became friends.

Now, in the evenings they all gather together by the banks of the laughing river, beneath the beautiful mountain, and they sing and dance and play their new song.

And the music floats over the river and echoes off of the great mountain top.

"I greet you with my mind,
I greet you with my lips,
I greet you with my heart,
and I have no weapons."

"I greet you with my mind, I greet you with my lips,
I greet you with my heart, and I have no weapons."

BUILDING YOUR DRUM

Step 1. Decorate frame

Use pens, glitter glue, cut-out pictures, and/or paints. Make it show something about you.

Step 2. Wrap first layer

Wrap tape around the top piece of wood. Don't stretch the tape yet. Pull tape out to below bottom piece of wood. **Now** stretch and lay the tape around the bottom wood and pull tight.

Step 3. Wrap entire drum

Turn frame over and continue to wrap and overlap the tape until the entire drum face is covered.

Step 4. Decorate face of drum

Use pens, paint and/or glitter glue to make a design on the face of your drum.

Step 5. Wrap second layer

Turn your drum and wrap a second layer over your first, going in the opposite direction.

Step 6. Decorate and wrap your mallet

If you wish, decorate your mallet to match your drum. It will look great! To protect your drum skin, wrap the mallet head with masking tape.

Drum Parts List
4 pieces 10" x 1⅜" x ½" wood
40 ft. of 2" wide cellophane tape
9" x ½" diameter wood dowel

Photographs of Ms.Vega by Larry Gaddis, Studio 49

PLAYING YOUR DRUM

Step 1. Hold drum in one hand, mallet in the other.

Step 2. Strike middle of drum with mallet.
(Sounds like **doom**)

Step 3. Strike rim of drum with mallet.
(Sounds like **tec**)

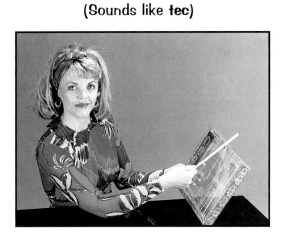

Step 4. Strike the flat edge of the drum rim with mallet.
(Sounds like **tac**)

Step 5. Tap finger on back of drum using hand that holds drum. Don't use mallet.
(Sounds like **da**)

Step 6. Experiment: how many sounds can you make?

Now you have four sounds. Let's make up some patterns. Using the four beats, try the following patterns. Then repeat them.

1. doom □ da □ tec-tec □ doom □ tec-tec
2. doom □ tac □ doom-doom □ tec
3. doom □ doom □ tec-tec □ doom

Be creative. How else can you. . .
> hold the drum?
> beat the drum?

Can you. . .
> use two mallets?
> change the pitch?
> play loud and soft?
> mute the beat?

WELCOME SONG MOTIONS

Do these motions while standing. Bend your knees on the beat of the music.

Touch head

I greet you with my mind

Touch lips

I greet you with my lips

Cross arms over chest

I greet you with my heart

Swing arms out and back, crossing in front of you

And I have no weapons

CHE, CHE, KOOLAY MOTIONS

Touch head

Che, che koolay (echo)

Touch shoulders

Che, che, ko, fe, sa (echo)

Touch chest

Ko fe salanga (echo)

Touch knees

Ga, ga shelanga (echo)

Rock side to side

Kum, eh, deh, deh (echo)
Kum, eh, deh, deh (echo)
Kum, eh, deh, deh (echo)

Clap

(altogether, clap)
Kum, kum, kum

DANCE INSTRUCTIONS (for the Funga Alafia Song)

There are three movements in this dance: (#1) Step-Close-Step, arms open and close; (#2) Jump and turn around; (#3) Rock side to side, clap twice. The dance uses these steps to make patterns. The first movement is to the right and then to the left.

(**Hint:** When you change directions, touch only your toe — not your whole foot — to the ground). So, moving to the right, it's . . . Step—Close—Step—Touch; then reverse direction to the left . . . Step—Close—Step—Touch.

MOVEMENT #1

(Always step to the right first).

1. Step right.
4. Step left.

2. Close.
5. Close.

3. Step right.
6. Step left.

MOVEMENT #2

(*See directions below).

1. Jump and turn around.

2. Repeat Movement #1

3. Jump and turn around

*In Movement #2 we add a jump on the word Funga. Always jump with your feet in an open position so you can close them on the next beat. So, it's Jump—Close—Step—Touch [Reverse direction] Step—Close—Step—Touch. Then repeat the movement.

DANCE INSTRUCTIONS (continued)

MOVEMENT #3

In the third movement, add a clap on the word **Alafia** and a rocking motion on the words **Áshe, Áshe**. So it's . . . Jump—Bounce—Clap—Clap—Rock(left)—Rock(right)—Rock(left)—Rock(right).

1. Jump. Bounce.

2. Clap. Clap.

3. Rock left.

4. Rock right.

Practice:

To practice these dance steps, stand alone in your own space.

(1) Practice Movement #1. Move to the right, Step—Close—Step—Close. Keep moving to the right until this is easy for you; then reverse direction and move to the left. Remember to touch with your toe, not your whole foot.

(2) When you can do these steps alone, try them with a line of people.

(3) When you can do these steps in a line, try them with two lines of people facing each other.

(4) Then do the steps with a circle of people.

(5) Then do the steps with two circles facing each other.

(6) Add Movement #2 — Jump.

(7) Add Movement #3 — Clap.

Patterns by song verses:

Verse 1 — Step—Close—Step—Touch; [Reverse] Step—Close—Step—Touch.

Verse 2 — Jump—Close—Step—Touch; [Reverse] Step—Close—Step—Touch.

Verse 3 — Jump—Bounce—Clap—Clap—Rock—Rock—Rock—Rock;
[Reverse] Jump—Bounce—Clap—Clap—Rock—Rock —Rock—Rock.

NOTE: For all verses, repeat the pattern twice.

Resources

Aremu, P.S.O. "Yoruba Traditional Weaving: Kijipa Motifs, Colour and Symbols," **Nigeria Magazine** 140, pp. 3—10.

Lamb, V. and J. **Nigerian Weaving**. Hertingfordbury, Roxford: Holmes, 1980.

Lloyd, P.C. **The Yoruba, An Urban People?** New York: Oxford Press, 1973.

Renne, Elisha P. **Water, Spirits and Plain White Cloth: The Ambiguity of Things in Bunu Social Life**, Australian National University.

Thompson, Robert Farris. **Flash of the Spirit. Áshe, The Power to Make Things Happen.** New York: Random House Inc., 1983.

Waterman, Christopher A. "Popular Music and the Construction of Pau-Yoruba Indentity," **Ethnomusicology**, Fall. University of Washington, 1990.

OTHER CHILDREN'S BOOKS BY RAYVE PRODUCTIONS

CHILDREN'S MULTICULTURAL BOOKS — Toucan Tales series

Entertaining and educational children's books featuring intriguing folktales with exquisite watercolor paintings set in different cultures around the world

Nekane, the Lamiña & the Bear
A tale of the Basque Pyrenees
by Frank P. Araujo, PhD ▪ illustrations by Xiao Jun Li
ISBN 1-877810-01-0 ▪ LC# 93-84620 ▪ 10½x9 ▪ Hardcover
32 pages ▪ 1993 ▪ $16.95 ▪ Full color
In English with pronunciation guide and
glossary for Basque words.
Toucan Tales
Volume 1

The Perfect Orange
A tale from Ethiopia   Toucan Tales Volume 2
by Frank P. Araujo, PhD ▪ illustrations by Xiao Jun Li
ISBN 1-877810-94-0 ▪ LC# 94-67524 ▪ 10½x9 ▪ Hardcover ▪ 32 pages
1994 ▪ $16.95 ▪ Full color
In English with pronunciation guide and glossary for Ethiopian words.

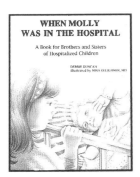

CHILDREN'S MEDICALLY ORIENTED
MINIMED SERIES — VOLUME 1

When Molly Was in the Hospital
A book for brothers and sisters of hospitalized children

by Debbie Duncan ▪ illustrations by Nina Ollikainen, MD
A special book for all those who care about children who are ill . . . and their families. The black and white illustrations are sensitively rendered and rich with details.
ISBN 1-877810-44-4 ▪ LC# 94-67525 ▪ 8x10 ▪ B/W hardcover ▪ 40 pages ▪ 1994 ▪ $12.95

RAYVE PRODUCTIONS INC.
BOX 726
WINDSOR CA 95492
ORDER (800)852-4890